Just in Case

What people are saying about Laura's fiction

I'm one of Laura McHale Holland's big fans. Her stories are edgy, chilling, laugh-out-loud, make you cry and always emotionally charged. I've had the pleasure of reading her entire collection, and ... all I can say is keep 'em coming.

— Ana Manwaring, author of *Set Up: Secrets and Lies in Zihuatanejo*

Holland's superbly imaginative prose probes a deeper understanding of the human condition and touches tender, guarded places in our hearts. Her memorable characters explore hidden layers of existence, some beyond the grave or across parallel planes.

— Nancy Pogue LaTurner, author of *Voluntary Nomads*

I know there is not such a thing as "surrealistic realism," although Laura McHale Holland's book of flash fiction did elicit that term from me as I devoured her characters, unsettling but yet inspiring ... with lots of just plain folks in images of love, hate and wonderment, and it goes on, until the last story when a soft whisper of "wow" escaped my lips.

— Linda Loveland Reid, author of *Touch of Magenta* and *Something in Stone*

Here are ordinary men and women as well as those who are insane, children, animals and ghosts–all taking part in this diurnal and nocturnal theater of the wonderful, dark and absurd. Diverse in subject, form and nature, these condensed stories are worth reading and rereading, so that one might savor the many layers of meaning, mystery and relatable humanity.

— Yu-Han Chao, author of *We Grow Old*

Modern fables with ... layers of meaning hidden in metaphor, revealed in raw emotion and haunting in their sudden intimacy.

— Kate Farrell, editor of the *Wisdom Has a Voice* anthology

Laura McHale Holland's stories are elegant, eerily haunting and often beautiful.

— Sunny Lockwood, author of *Shades of Love*

JUST IN CASE

twenty-one bite-sized stories

Laura McHale Holland

ISBN paperback: 978-1-7336683-0-9
ISBN ebook: 978-1-733-6683-1-6
Library of Congress control number: 2019909079

Certain stories in this book were previously published as follows:

"Drifting," *The Ice Cream Vendor's Song,* 2012
"Hare Speaks," *Everyone Likes a Good Fairy Tale anthology,* Sitting Room, 2018
"Invasion," *Every Day Fiction Three,* 2011
"Open Range," Healdsburg Center for the Arts, Elizabeth Wonnacott exhibit, 2015
"When She Wakes Up," *The Ice Cream Vendor's Song,* 2012

Cover design by Rena Hoberman, Cover Quill
Book design by Jo-Anne Rosen, Wordrunner Press
Author photo by Jason Figueroa

Contents

For my beautiful granddaughters,
Ava Kate and Reina Elizabeth:
May stories always bring you magic.

Introduction

Imagine a world where shadows of enchantment instantly render ordinary experiences eerie, terrifying or sublime, and where the unexpected becomes the norm. The twenty-one micro stories in Laura McHale Holland's *Just in Case* comprise such a place: a universe where a wife betrayed relishes her revenge; a couple chugging toward retirement takes a surprising U-turn; a much maligned character finally has his say; a cozy family scene chills the blood; a curious relative cannot leave a half-human baby alone. These, and more, are what you'll find in this book.

Red

Six-year-old Tessie held a basket of ruby-red rose petals in hands so moist the wicker handle almost slid from her fingers. Mommy was a breath behind.

"Don't let me down, now," Mommy said before nudging Tessie forward. But the girl's feet were boulders, her arms petrified wood. She willed herself to lift the petals and drizzle them as she walked—just like she'd done during rehearsal—but she could not.

Nor could she look ahead or even to the side. She could only peer down at her pink Mary Janes, as she thought of the last time she saw her daddy. They were at a bus station, she with nose to pane, he waving from the sidewalk as the bus pulled away, Mommy in the aisle seat, saying, "It's just us now. Be a big girl. Don't let me down."

Tessie's lips puckered as she trod down the aisle. She knew she was doing it wrong, knew the petals were supposed to be in a trail behind her, knew she was letting Mommy down. She glanced at the man whose eyes she'd been avoiding. The man at the altar. New person. New daddy. New smile not meant for her. Not really.

She pressed on. The white teeth, the kindly eyes, the immaculate tuxedo growing closer, larger. Still she could not move her arms. Until, finally, inches from the altar, her arms took control, turned her burden upside down, and dumped the petals in one crimson cascade. She threw the basket to the side and dashed to her assigned seat. An auntie she barely knew pulled her close, wrapped long arms around her, and said she'd done a fine job.

Tessie sank into the folds of the woman's satin dress and peeked out at Mommy, a vision in an off-white gown with a border of tiny violets. She knew better than to make eye contact. Mommy's beautiful face would say it all as she stepped over the pile on the carpet, red as Tessie's sorrow, red as her love for Daddy, red as her flushing cheeks.

Just in Case

Dan's gone. Two years now. The kids, scattered far, never visit. They say it's my fault. Didn't I know something was wrong? Life throws crazy curves. I count my blessings: little home paid off, little pension, little dog snuggled at my feet, little pistol in hand just in case I want to go too.

Hare Speaks

Hare here. Yes, the long-eared bugger everyone chides because Tortoise beat me in one silly race. Okay, I admit I was puffed up, a walking ego, a not very nice guy. If I'd been a kid on your playground, I'd have bullied you a time or two. But I wouldn't say I was ever malicious.

You've read the fable, right? You know the gist of it. I boasted of my speed and prowess. All. The. Time. Now, that alone may have been tolerable, but I made fun of Tortoise, too, made him feel less-than. This finally ticked him off, and he challenged me to a race. Crazy right?

I thought it would be an easy win. What hare in his right mind wouldn't? But from the start, I shot so far ahead, I became over-confident, scatterbrained, or both, depending on how you spin the tale. I dawdled, thinking poor Tortoise would never catch up. Plus, what fun would it have been if I'd just bounded at top speed to the finish? No, I had to taunt him, let him think he had a chance—then dash his hopes in style.

But, as you know, the upset was stunning. I live on in infamy, because people love to root for the underdog. Face it. Most of us have, at times, felt like threes on a scale of one to ten. And only a fraction of us actually are tens. We're fives or sixes, maybe sevens. So a story about a humble tortoise besting a bumptious hare has legs. It offers hope.

So take your encouragement from this tale if you must. Chant, "Slow and steady wins the race" as you go through your days. There's good in that.

But here's the thing: life is a series of crossroads with new choices to make. Who's to say I didn't learn from my mistakes? If Tortoise and I raced again, which could easily happen if I goaded him, and if I became my true self, a focused speed demon, which is likely because I am not stupid, after all; everyone's favorite reptile would be left wallowing in mud and never challenge me again. He'd have to create a new motto, too, something like, "Stay in your lane" or "Do what you're good at." For Tortoise, that might be sunning on a log, and I guess there's not much of a story in that.

Suspended Wonder

Houseboats moored in the bay. The city, by turns cloaked in morning fog, or shimmering in sunlight so sublime you squeezed my arm to make sure we weren't in a dream. We sped back and forth in our Corolla, enchanted by visions of redwood cathedrals, seals barking on the Farallons, sand dollars on the beach. We thrilled at the sight of headlands rising, the luscious landscapes unfolding beyond. And there was the bridge itself, an engineering marvel, a suspended wonder.

Didn't we want to see it up close? We'd driven it countless times but never walked the span. It was about time, we said, and chose a day so brisk a gust tore away my favorite hat. Taupe, polished cotton, with a two-inch brim and a clump of plastic cherries that looked sweet enough to eat as the hat twirled down to choppy water.

The wind calmed. We held hands and walked on, eager to traverse the landmark at long last, knowing we could savor the views for as long as we liked. But with each step the urge to linger faded. You wheezed, snorted. I sniffed, coughed. You pulled a handkerchief from your pocket to dab my watering eyes. I put my palms on your chest and tucked in, gagging. All the while cars, trucks, vans, buses and motorcycles burped, groaned and rattled along.

Suddenly, I wished to follow the hat, to escape from a civilization always barging through, never still enough to embrace peace. I wrenched away and leaned over the rail, wondering whether I'd die on impact as I extended my hands into the salt air. You stretched down and touched your cheek to mine. "It's all about compromise," you whispered.

Cold Case

Of course it was a witch we outsmarted in the woods, not some feeble, senile neighbor. And yes, her home was built of candy and cake. Impossible? I have no time for people who don't believe in magic. I am not a sociopath. She was about to eat my brother—me next, no doubt. You think the jewels make us look guilty, that it was all premeditated? You think we killed our stepmom, too? Outrageous! You have no proof. Hansel made a deal? He'll never testify against me. Let's just see what a jury has to say.

Nephew

"A blasted curse," Zoe complained as she forced the writhing bundle into Betsy's arms. "Just get it out of here."

Betsy jiggled the baby and gawked at her big sister, who shoved bloodied towels and rags into a trash bag. The birth had been a battlefield—intense and gory. Betsy couldn't fathom how Zoe had endured it in silence.

"Go on. You know what to do." Zoe's impatience spread like turpentine on a wound.

"Are you really sure?"

"We've been over this, like, a thousand times. Go, get out of here before the thing starts crying again," Zoe snapped. "You've got to do the dump fast and get right home."

"But the cleanup, it's such—"

"I'll take care of this. You've got to hurry. It was easy enough to hide my weight gain with baggy clothes. Mom's so preoccupied all the time." Disdain stiffened Zoe's face as she pointed to the baby. "But there's no way I can hide that. And Mom can't know." Her voice quavered. "She'd always hold it against me."

With thoughts jumbled like dice in a shaker, Betsy carried her nephew three blocks to Fire Station No. 3, where her seventh-grade class had taken a field trip a few weeks ago. The captain was tall and solid with a superhero voice. At the entrance, Betsy knelt and placed the babe on a gray rubber mat, averting her eyes from the life just begun. She rose and turned to walk away, staving off a confusion of feelings with clenched teeth. She took a step toward the sidewalk, hoping the captain would be the one to find him. The boy could do worse than be greeted by a hero, she thought.

Then a tiny whimper cracked her resolve. She returned to her nephew and took him into her arms. After peeling the blanket from his face, she looked into his deep blue eyes and said, "Welcome to this big, fat, complicated world, kiddo." Then she reached up and rang the bell, certain her sister would never forgive her. Heart pounding, she listened as footsteps inside drew near.

Open Range

Ned shoves a box of kitchen utensils into the back of the Volvo wagon, closes the door and gazes at the fuchsia bougainvillea climbing his homemade trellis one last time before he walks to the driver's door.

"That's all of it then," his wife, Rosie, says when he gets in.

"Guess so." Ned starts the engine and steers the car down the drive and into the street.

Empty nesters—he riddled with arthritis, she with glaucoma—they just sold their home of forty years and are on their way to Morningside Estates, a community for senior citizens. Rosie waves to a neighbor walking two brown-and-white Chihuahuas as they drive by.

"I'll tell you something, Ned, I'm not

going to miss those yappy little dogs," she says.

Ned rounds the corner and heads toward the highway. "Never was much of a neighborly neighborhood, if you ask me," he says.

"How could it be with everybody at work all the time?"

"A ghost town, really." Ned turns onto the highway.

"Lots of poppies this year, oh, and look at Debbie Swan's lavender!"

"It's a purple lake, Rosie, a purple lake."

"And beyond that, the open range, love, with wild horses running free."

"What? Oh, yeah, the riding academy. I always liked that palomino."

"It's open range today, not some two-bit riding school."

"Like our future, open range."

"Like the free range chickens we never raised."

"And the horses we never rode." Ned's eyes tear up.

"Can we stop at Trader Joe's up ahead? I want to pick up a few things."

"You don't have to cook anymore, you know."

"We'll still have a kitchen. Besides, I never made an olallieberry pie."

"I never rode that palomino either." He does a U-turn and floors it.

She braces herself, hands on dashboard. "What are you doing?"

"I'm gonna ride that horse, honey. I've got to ride that horse."

No Need

The barista was lithe as a panther—dangerous, too, with swiveling hips, cherry-colored lips and purple bangs framing bed-me eyes—a perfect temptress. Donna, furious after decades married to a rake, placed her order with the hussy: chai latte, his favorite.

Order rung up, the strumpet asked Donna for her name.

"Ralph." Donna teased her husband's name out slowly while watching a vein in the woman's temple throb.

The trollop raised an eyebrow and flashed a row of pointed teeth, looking more like a cornered rat than a regal feline now.

The urge to poke harder engulfed Donna like a sinkhole swallowing a road. "That's Ralph Hanley," she said. Her feigned sweetness threatened like a knife.

The barista's cheek twitched in time to the throbbing temple as she wrote the name on a cup and forced a yawn in an attempt to relax her jaw.

Donna exited, no need for a drink.

Down to the Beach

Willa parked at the cove, a sheltered spot Nate never liked. "You're such a wimp," he'd say whenever she suggested they go there. He liked beaches where the wind whipped so hard it made your ears burn. That didn't matter now. He was gone, along with most of her belongings—even the Siamese cat he despised.

When she dipped her toes into the surf, few people populated the shore. A lean man threw a stick into the waves for his retriever, a wiggling, wagging boomerang that fetched again and again. A woman sat on a driftwood log, opened an umbrella, and spun it on her shoulder like a southern belle. On a bluff to the right, a boy and girl raced too close to the edge with a yipping white dog that spun circles around their feet.

Willa longed to be one with the water. She wanted to wade out, ease into the breaststroke and swim far from shore, let Nate have everything he hadn't managed to take already. She counted under her breath, preparing to carry out her plan, when the wind picked up, roiling the usually quiet cove. Waves rose swiftly, slapping her shins. She'd wanted a peaceful exit, not this. Then a sleeper wave lashed up, engulfed the little dog and swept it toward water churning around rocks large as elephants. "Billy! Billy Boy!" the children screamed.

Willa dove into the waves as the animal smacked the surface, but when she reached the point of impact, she saw no sign of him. Then up came his head. He yelped and thrashed. The ocean pulled him down. She lunged and caught him with her fingertips just in time.

He bit her. Hard. Bit her with everything he had. She laughed at the pain, laughed at the saltwater washing away blood, laughed

as she held him high for the children racing
across ice plant down to the beach.

Invasion

I heard her. I heard her talking all lovey-dovey to them after she didn't answer the phone, something that's happening way too often lately, if you ask me. She makes excuses when I mention it. She says, "Oh, I must have been asleep," or "I was visiting Nicole next door," or something like that. But this time I knew she was at home—and awake. I'd just ferried her back from a pedicure, seen her grab the railing and inch up her front stairs, wisps of gray sticking out from her black beret. So, I was worried when I called to ask what she wanted for dinner. I thought she might have gone out back and fallen off the ladder she's always climbing—against doctor's orders, mind you—nobody to spot her: my long-reluctant, lovely mother.

I ran over, cell phone in hand, ready to call 911; then I found her talking baby talk to that pack of raccoons, those dirty varmints. They've taken up residence outside her kitchen window, in her avocado tree, perched two or three to a branch, those raccoons. And now I know it's true. She talks to them rather than answer the phone. Nicole said so, said she leans her face in close to their masked eyes and sharp claws, too close. Every evening she babbles to them on and on. Tells them secrets.

I want to kill them, kill them all. Kill them so my mother will answer my calls, those vile, probably rabid creatures. Kill them all. They've stolen her mind; they're responsible. Before they took over that tree, before the invasion, at least I had hopes she'd smile at me, say my name, ask how my day went when I walk through her door. Hopes.

I need an accomplice, someone to distract her while I do the deed. But who? The little boy who lives up the street? She offers him candy every morning when he delivers the paper. It's the same fun-sized Butterfinger bar leftover from last Halloween. Day after day, the same piece of candy in her hand; the same, "No thank you, ma'am," coming from him. Has he told his mom about her?

It's only a matter of time before someone insists she be sent away; I can't watch her every minute, even though I live on the block and spend as much time with her as I can. That nosy graduate student who drops by every week with a jar of homemade pesto might set the ball rolling, maybe, or the mailman who's always pestering her to trim her rosebush hedge, even though I do it myself twice a year. Or her doctor could any day just say it's time; let her go, let her go.

Oh, let's face it. I can't kill even one raccoon, let alone a tree full of them. Animal control will have to cart them away in cages. She should make the call; it's her property. But she'll never do it. My dear, distracted, demented mother, Mom, Mommy, Ma, the Old Lady, and her new family or whatever you want to call them, those raccoons. She loves them. She loves them. She's even named them, each and every one. She thinks she can tell them apart.

And the thing is tomorrow or the next day or next month when her signals sputter and cross, when she forgets, when she can't tell which one is which, when she mixes up their names, even calls one of them her own name, or when she thinks she's seeing them for the first time, when she does all that, their feelings won't be hurt. They'll carry on with their raccoon ways, eating, climbing up and down the branches, looking like they know something I don't, like it's all a big joke anyway.

Names. What do names mean to them? They only mean something to me, the one she swaddled but never embraced. The one who makes sure the bills are paid, the floor is mopped. The one who cuts her roast beef sandwiches into half-inch squares and forks them one by one into her mouth as she watches "Judge Judy" repeats on TV.

The one whose name wobbles at the back of her tongue, all too soon to slide down her throat, never to be spoken again.

Murky Water

She kicks gravel by the pond. A step away, he gazes at a lavender moon. Their fingertips touch, separate, touch again. She stuffs her hands into silk-lined pockets. "So, this is it, then," she says.

His hand turns, palm up—an invitation. "Doesn't seem right," he says, "you leavin' me."

"But you love her; you told me so." She pivots away.

"Don't be that way," he says. "It happens, that's all, like amethyst moon glow, fish flip-flapping, pebbles underfoot. Means nothing."

She steals into the purple night, soothed by falling forest leaves. He curses murky water. Koi flee.

Drag Me Home

She erased my mind before thoughts even formed words. The interminable assault of emotions, slap of paddles, force-feeding of lies, love irreparably scorched drove me away.

Silent screams rose from diaphragm to forehead, reverberating as I marched, blighted, into adulthood.

Thousands of blocks and miles; numerous mountains, plains, plateaus, forests, thickets, brooks, streams and rivers; endless roads, byways, highways, expressways and freeways; myriad ranches, subdivisions, mansions, apartments, schools and universities; countless country clubs, restaurants, drive-ins, coffee shops, bakeries, chain stores, boutiques, hotels, motels and seedy dives—all between us—held her at bay.

During drab days of repetitive tasks in monochrome offices, I struggled to reclaim a person who had never been allowed to exist, all the while haunted by beady eyes peering through my dreams, attempting to snare me and drag me home. I grew strong as a weed whose roots could not be pulled.

Drifting

She is a rainbow fading as she loads the laundry. He is an old Chevy idling on the couch. He sees a brilliant arch of color turning as she reaches for the Tide. She turns toward him and sees a fast ride down a dirt road on a long-ago sunburned evening.

She shakes the detergent box and hears seashell and driftwood chimes. She pours the powder into the washer, closes the lid, turns the dial. The machine rumbles; the waterfall comes.

"What would you like for lunch?" she asks.

The coffee table is a creaking pier, the carpet a beach of turquoise sand. "I think I'd like ..."

He closes his eyes and becomes a boat drifting in a leather sea. She sits in the rocker facing him. She rocks. She rocks. She rocks and becomes the wind. She becomes the wind blowing him to shore. He opens his eyes.

"What would you like for lunch?" she asks.

Talisman

Jory wore a screaming-orange sweater when he left for Bali. We took pictures at the airport, our little gang of thirty-something theater majors. Returning students we were called. Each of us wore something zany. I sported an oversize, multicolored beret. Around her neck, Susan wrapped an angora scarf—six feet long, lavender and softer than a cotton ball. Ted wore a lime-green ascot and tweed jacket with holes at the elbows. Brian pranced in cowboy boots trimmed with mother of pearl. All were flea market finds. Jory insisted they were talismans that protected us from the traps of ordinary concerns. We believed him, cheering to that notion nightly over beers at the Rite Spot.

The vacation of his dreams is what Jory called it the June day he departed. Six weeks in paradise. Then he'd be back to enchant us with stories as we readied for a new semester. But he didn't return as planned. He sent us a postcard instead. He declared his life was now a theater performance. How could university classes compare?

No matter how much we rehearsed after that, our scenes on stage were flat as blank paper. We gathered a few times at the Rite Spot, laughed at things we no longer found funny, confided how empty classes were without him, how suspended our lives. We tucked away our dreams along with our flea market clothes—temporarily, each of us said, certain he'd come home soon to ignite and unite us again.

Living in separate cities now, we keep in touch on Facebook. Ted saw it first: a video gone viral of an expat in Bali who stepped in front of an oncoming truck to push a fallen child to safety. The man was wrinkled with scraggly salt-and-pepper hair, his neon orange sweater unmistakable as the bumper thrust him into the air. Our talisman gone.

Before

The scene glowed cozy. Fire in pot-bellied stove. Calico kittens romping on braided rug. Chocolate chip cookies cooling on plate. Hot cocoa in ruby-red mugs. A mother reading The Runaway Bunny to three sleepy tots. I took it all in before turning off the power.

I'll Have To Tell Him

My Bernie's a real good man, except he gets these harebrained ideas. I try my darnedest to put the kibosh on them—like befriending Jake the Wolfman. We called him that 'cause he kept wolves, well, not really wolves, but wolf dogs—half wolf, half dog—which some folks say are worse than wolves because they have instincts pointing them every which way.

I didn't take to the idea of the Wolfman, but my Bernie's the most curious guy in all of North Bend, and the friendliest, too. He's a mail carrier, and he got this route a few years back that included Jake the Wolfman's spread. They started by sayin' hi, and then a few friendly words, you know, how's the wife doin' or those sure are pretty critters you have there. Pretty soon Bernie was savin' Jake the Wolfman's mail till last and then shootin' the breeze on his front porch for an hour or so before comin' home, which I didn't appreciate, and I told Bernie so.

But, you know, I couldn't stay mad about it because Bernie has this sheepish grin that gets to me, so he can get away with anything, darn it. And after a while I guess I started to look forward to his stories about what was new with Jake the Wolfman because, let's face it, things are pretty boring here in North Bend—just lots of us sittin' around with nothin' to do and nothin' but dreams left of jobs that went south of the border or to Asia or wherever.

So Jake the Wolfman had about a dozen of 'em in a big enclosure, about four acres. And he went in there and ran around with them, said the wolf dogs were his brothers. He tried to get Bernie to go in with him. Bernie swears he never did because a dozen of them crazy wolf dogs was just too much for him. But he did say one-on-one those wolf dogs were as sweet as can be and a little mysterious, too, like something out of a myth. I told him right then and there that was a big bunch of hooey. Oh, but Bernie looked so stricken by my words, I wished I could have taken 'em back.

Then Bernie came home one day real down in the dumps. He flopped on his recliner and sat starin' at the TV, which wasn't even on, mind you. And I said, Bernie, what in the dickens has gotten into you, and he grunted a little but couldn't get a word out for a long time, but I kept askin', and finally he said those wolf dogs had up and killed Jake the Wolfman.

Bernie said an ambulance was driving away when he pulled up in the mail van, and police and animal control officers and even North Bend's fire captain were swarming around the property. Dead wolf dogs were stacked in a pile just inside the enclosure, and Bernie saw a pool of blood at the gate. There were a lot of tears that night between the two of us, I'll tell you. Bernie was sobbing, and I was cryin' for

Bernie, and then I was wailin' for Jake the Wolfman, even though I didn't even know him. And I was cryin' about maybe having to let go of a fantasy Bernie had, and I was starting to have, too, about things being different than they really are between people and wild animals.

We were still weepy the next morning when Bernie went off to work. I expected we'd be glum at the end of the day, too. But Bernie returned at suppertime with that sheepish grin of his and a big bulge in his jacket. I asked, what's in there, but he kept mum. He sat in his chair, unzipped the jacket, and there were two little pups, couldn't have been more than eight weeks old. He'd gone to Jake the Wolfman's house, sat on the front porch to just think about his pal, and he heard squealing coming from the direction of the enclosure. He went inside and found the pups huddled way back in a corner behind a pile of bricks.

Bernie asked me if he could keep them. He looked so hopeful, and the pups looked so cute snuggled there in the chair. I said okay. I said it real stern, like a cop, so as not to let on how adorable I thought the little critters were. I insisted these half-wild animals live out back in the yard, though, for our own peace of mind. Bernie said he was okay with that.

We built a doghouse out back and told the neighbors our pups are sled-dog mutts, so everything is cool with them. Each day Bernie feeds them their breakfast kibble before he goes off to work. When he leaves, I wave goodbye from the front door. Then I bring the babies inside. I never expected to turn into a wolf-person. But when I look into their blue eyes, I know they understand me in ways not even Bernie does. My Bernie. Pretty soon I'll have to tell him about the pups and me because, well, two of them babies just isn't enough.

Believe Me

Alina swooshed in and flounced onto the bed. "Look, Herb! Footprints, tiny footprints in the snow." She waved her iPhone in front of his face.

He groaned, eyes closed.

"They're real footprints. I captured them."

He opened his eyes, scratched his head with both hands. "Shouldn't you be at work by now? You open the store today, right?"

"I'll be a few minutes late. Who cares? There's no reason for me to open a bookstore at 8:30 a.m. Nobody ever comes in before 10."

"You're lucky to have that job, remember? I shouldn't have to remind you how important it is for you to have something to do again."

"I know you and that high-priced Marlee therapist person both think I'm crezy, but look!" She inched closer to him. "You'll have to believe me once you see this picture."

He rolled onto his back, stretched, then put his arms behind his head and leaned against a pillow. "Can't you just try to move on? We're all doing our best."

"But look." She waved the phone again. "See? Footprints in the snow. Toddler-size footprints."

Herb took hold of the device and breathed slowly as he studied the photo from several angles. "Could be an optical illusion, a play on light, something like that, kind of like those bogus miracles people see, like the face of Jesus on a piece of toast, you know?"

"I heard crying outside the window. It was our Tommy. I'd know his voice anywhere. I brushed aside the curtain just in time to see a shadow, his shadow, round the corner. I don't know why he didn't wait for me. I wish he had, but those footprints, they're a sign."

He handed the phone back to her, shaking his head. "You're seeing what you want to see."

"The same's true of you and that creepy Marlee. I'm not going back to her."

He rose from the bed. "I lost him, too, you know, but I'm not going to let it ruin me. You shouldn't either." He padded to the bathroom.

Alina stared at the photo. The footprints were as clear to her as her bitten fingernails. Herb started the shower. From the attic came peals of laughter so familiar, so dear. What has brought Tommy such joy? she wondered, and ran for the stairs.

Keeping to Yourself

We are boring, my dad and I. People don't say it to our faces, but I know it's true. We can't converse. We're not interested in much. We don't let anyone know how we feel—not even ourselves, which could be why Mom left us eons ago, back when I was maybe ten years old and the spittin' image of Dad, so she said.

But now there's something interesting happening, a bit frightening even, right here on my old Toshiba laptop. I'm trying to type a run-of-the-mill email to Dad's doctor because he's been in bed for a couple of days and starting to stink, like old folks tend to do. I finished the salutation, you know, "Hi Dr. Baker," when the computer heated up like an iron. Then I lost control. Someone or something took over and wrote terrible things about me—some sort of confession.

Now, on one hand, this is exciting. Nothing like this ever happens to boring old me. On the other hand, the thing is in my lap and getting so hot, I'm afraid it's going to burn right through my jeans. And what is Dr. Baker going to think if whatever has taken over presses Send? It's typing that I never loved my dad, can't stand the sight of him, never want to see him again, have wanted him gone for a long time. Word after word of pure b.s.

I have to put a stop to this. What can I do? Ah, okay, I'll slam the machine shut. Ouch! It hurts to touch. Oh, oh, I have to get it off of me. Throw it off. Oh no! It landed on Dad's bed, and it's glowing red like a giant coal. How can that be? And there's fire now, and smoke, smoke all around me. I'll jump out the window. No other way. Dad's so still. No time to worry about him. I'm choking. Can't breathe. Gotta get out.

Whew! I've landed in those thorny rose bushes Dad loves so much. Okay, so I'm a little scratched up. Gadzooks! The house! It's exploding. I'm running, running to the sidewalk, running with bricks and boards flying by my head. Can you believe it? My ears are ringing something awful. Neighbors are milling about, asking if I'm okay, wanting to know what happened. I can't tell the truth. I'll say Dad fell asleep while smoking in bed. That's perfect. Only I know whether or not he smoked. There are advantages in keeping to yourself.

No One To See

The girl was ill prepared for severe. Overbearing, scattered, raucous—all things foreign to her—she could have adapted to those qualities in a guardian. But in her new home, severe was a living, breathing force all its own, siphoning off hope.

Wake up to severe, wash face, brush teeth, eat breakfast to severe staring as though she were a gnat, as though she could be junked with one slap. Who wouldn't cringe? Run home from school, knee skinned, to rage-infested hands scraping flesh, pouring iodine, eyes glinting with satisfaction at pain sharp as scissors slicing scrap from stars. Who wouldn't float between thoughts?

The child grew slant, stashing poems behind attic chests, in coat linings, under ornaments, in creased photo albums, encyclopedias, cookbooks—days to months to years.

With toes snug in scuffed loafers, the girl tiptoed away. She joined a swell of youth, each one a prism with tales to tell. Severe haunted the guardian, who found little papers tucked here and there; with each stanza, a grizzled heart softened, no one to see.

Butterflies

One week after fourteen-year-old Lena went missing, a yellow suitcase appeared in front of her locker. Paula recognized it but pretended not to. It was the first day of spring. She wanted to celebrate, not worry about Lena or remember the long-ago play dates, the fantasy games the girls played with props and costumes stored in that case. She wanted to forget Lena's obsession with the iridescent purple and turquoise butterfly wings leftover from Halloween when they were seven years old. Paula was a butterfly that year, too, but she lost interest in her costume, crammed it in her closet, and didn't object when her mom carted her wings to Goodwill a few years later.

Lena's fixation deepened through the years. By the time they entered middle school, all of Lena's clothes incorporated butterflies in the design. She drew the insects all over her assignments and tests instead of doing the work. And she spoke only of butterflies. Paula finally broke away from Lena. It was a relief: no more teasing, no more wicked jokes. At first, she felt pangs of guilt when she saw Lena walk down the halls alone, dodging taunts classmates hurled at her. But she'd managed to banish thoughts of her former friend, that is, until Lena disappeared.

Paula kicked the suitcase, angry at Lena for being weird and for disappearing. She kicked it again. A few friends joined in. A crowd gathered. Excitement spread as adolescents took turns whacking and stomping. Faculty members approached, intending to disperse the group and send them to class. Paula gave the suitcase one more whack. It broke open. Out flew hundreds of iridescent butterflies. The winged beauties swept around the group, mesmerizing all, and then flew right through the wall of lockers. Paula and her classmates chased after them, slipping easily through the wall. A few of the teachers tried to follow, but they were met with solid locker doors.

Soon, the police arrived, parents, too. Witnesses shared stories. Various theories were discussed. But there were no leads. The grief-stricken community tore down the school and replaced it with a garden. No one goes near.

When She Wakes Up

My niece Emma's a little different. It started after a family rafting trip turned tragic when she was twelve. Her mom, dad and brother all drowned when the raft overturned. Emma was found downstream hours later, badly bruised but alive.

When she came to live with me right after that, all Emma could talk about was how one of those Bigfoot creatures had plunged into the rapids and saved her. I did my best to bring her down gently to the reality that it's fun to tell stories about Bigfoot sightings around campfires, but only crackpots believe they actually exist.

Emma never did accept my point of view on that, though, or on much of anything else either. And when she finished high school she went to live in the woods way up north in Humboldt County instead of going to college. Like I said, she's a little different.

Last week she called and asked if she could come for a visit. I said yes, of course. Then she said she'd just had a baby girl with her boyfriend and she was bringing the baby, too. She said her boyfriend wasn't coming though because he hates to travel. Well, I didn't even know she had a boyfriend, let alone a baby. But that doesn't matter. I was thrilled to see her and the baby when they arrived this morning. The tyke was all wrapped up and sleeping, though. Emma was tired, too, so they went to take a nap in Emma's old room.

Before she fell asleep Emma told me that if the baby cried, to just leave her alone—no matter what. But a little while ago, the little one started sobbing, and it tore at my heart. I decided to tend to her. That way Emma could keep on sleeping.

I tiptoed into the room and picked up the babe. She was wiggling and wailing so hard I thought, what harm could it do to loosen the blanket a bit and uncover the baby's face so she could get some air? But as soon as I lifted the blanket flap, I felt no more weight in my arms. I saw no face, no body. The blanket held only silence, stillness.

I put the blanket down by Emma right where it had been and ran out of the room. My heart is still racing at the sight. I know I heard that baby crying, felt her squirm in my arms. Now, Emma's odd. I've always accepted that. But this goes way beyond anything I could have imagined. What on earth am I going to do when she wakes up?

Acknowledgments

I have so many people to thank for the life I enjoy today, which, happily, includes creative projects like this one. Recently, I received a package from a dear friend from high school. She had saved poems I wrote when I was seventeen. Through the decades she kept them tucked away and returned them to me because she thought I'd enjoy seeing them again. Rare and beautiful surprises like this add a magical sheen to my days. The kind deeds on the part of my sisters, Kathy and Mary Ruth; husband, Jim; children, Ryan, Jackson and Moira; and bitty granddaughter, Ava, are legion. Uncle John, dear Unc, gave me unconditional love for every one of the ninety-eight years he lived. And the astute, supportive, funny friends in my critique group, Skye, Patrice, Beth Ann and Marie, boost my spirits week after week. Ace editor Julie Fadda spots errors that slip by me. Performance poet Claire Blotter and master storyteller Ruth Stotter continue to believe in and inspire me. On evenings when I stumble over words and feel too tired to move, I think of all of these people, take another step, and then another. It is with tremendous appreciation for them that I carry on.

A Note to Readers

Thank you for reading this collection of flash fiction. If you like what you read, please sign up for my newsletter at https://laura-mchaleholland.com. I call my subscribers my "readers group" because it strikes me as more friendly than "subscribers," and it evokes the kind of interaction I'm interested in having with folks who like my work.

As a member, you will receive recently penned stories, previews of upcoming releases, special members-only offers and other news and reflections from my writing room.

Other than being willing to receive an email from me about once a month, nothing else will be required of you, although I will offer occasional opportunities to become involved in launches and special events for those who are interested.

Speaking of launches, an excerpt from my novel-in-progress follows the About page in this book. I hope you enjoy it. I will always be eager to receive your thoughts on what my work stirs up in you.

About The Author

I believe when we
follow our fondest
dreams, we open
doors for other kin-
dred souls. While
this is rarely easy,
and life wrench-
es without mercy

at times, words well-crafted can enchant,
mend and empower us to rejoice in our
hopes anew. This quest and the friendships
formed along the way are central to my
life and writing, through which I plumb
diverse emotions in memoir, fiction, poet-
ry and plays. My new novel, *The Kiminee
Dream*, introduces a cast of quirky, some-
times contentious characters in a fiction-
al town where enigmatic forces help and
hinder, and secrets surface, testing the

61

entire community's mettle. To learn more, visit https://lauramchaleholland.com, where you can read all about my award-winning books, as well as sign up to receive my newsletter, which, along with giving you special offers and updates on my writing life will, I hope, offer inspiration to help you reach for your own fondest dreams.

The Kiminee Dream

Laura McHale Holland

Prologue

In the town of Kiminee, the end was never the end, sorrow left supple scars and wishes cracked reality. This was true even when a teenager forced too soon into womanhood darted through a moonlit winter night, exhaling moist clouds into biting air. Clad in a sleeveless, cotton nightgown and slippers worn thin, the young fan of frilly dresses, black roses and Bing Crosby's mellow baritone didn't wince at the cold. She ran on, eyes glazed with fever, dewy skin blemished.

At the riverbank, she vaulted over snow-covered boulders onto solid ice. With arms outstretched and face tilted skyward, she glided. Voice wavering, she rasped a lullaby her mother used to sing in a city where coal dust muted the horizon. Her heart thrummed. Tears flowed. Blood slid down her thighs.

She kicked up her feet. Gone were the slippers, replaced by skates of purest-white leather with gleaming blades; gone was the nightie, replaced by a costume with sequined rainbows and silver fringe. She leaped, spun, landed. Ice cracked. She rose and fell again. The brittle surface groaned. She leaped higher, higher—each time a creak, a crack. Into the air she twirled once more. When she touched down, a fissure welcomed her. She plummeted, lips closed, eyes smiling.

When she embraced her maker that frozen Illinois night in 1936, all residents of the community nestled along the river's curves were asleep. Except for one. And for decades to come, they knew nothing of her brief life and demise.

Except for one.

Chapter One

Carly Mae Foley came into the world much like any other babe in 1953. She wailed when a doctor spanked her bottom. Her woozy mother, Velda, croaked, "There you are," and then passed out. Damon, her father, raced from waiting room to nursery when he learned his newborn had arrived. Carly Mae's brother and sister, Ray and Blanche, flaxen-haired twins born one year to the day before her, dumped bowls of Cheerios from high chairs. They spoke in a secret language their grandmother, Missy Lake, mistook for babble as she pulled out her address book and dialed all her friends from her kitchen wall phone.

Soon Kiminee, Illinois—a town that had just grown from 1,256 to 1,257—was abuzz with the news, for whenever a new child arrived people and animals alike set aside their differences to celebrate as one joyous whole. It was the Kiminee way. Mothers jigged around kitchens. Children cartwheeled through the town square. Fathers belted show tunes in their fields. Pigs played kick the can with bobcats; chickens dined with hawks; rabbits napped with coyotes. For little Carly Mae, even the Bendy River got in the act, burbling a tune that sounded a lot like "You Are My Sunshine" while crawdads came out of hiding to march in formation along the banks. While everyone always returned to normal in a day or two, interest in each child's development remained keen. And it wasn't long before the auburn-tufted addition to the Foley family became something of a celebrity. "A wonder," "genuine genius," "one in a million" and "uncanny" were used to describe her, because in every developmental area, she did nothing but astound. She sang before she talked and danced before she walked. She read Charlotte's Web at age two, mastered multiplication at three and did long division in her head at four.

At five, she taught herself to tap dance up and down walls like Fred Astaire. When she turned six in July of 1959, she set up a lemonade stand that, in one summer, raised $70 to help families devastated by an inferno hundreds of miles away. The conflagration had killed scores of students. She'd learned of the tragedy months earlier on the TV news, and the thought of all those children who would never again run barefoot through grass made her heart quiver with grief. She posted signs to that effect at her lemonade stand, which could be why so many people gave her 10 cents for 5-cent lemonades and told her to keep the change. It also helped that the Illinois State Fair gave her a booth near the entrance on the busiest day of the year.

On a sunny Saturday when she was seven, Carly Mae was discovered. It happened while she was painting portraits of Buster, a thirty-pound, tricolor husky-sheltie cross with a lopsided grin and only one ear. The dog had arrived on the Foley family's doorstep as a scrawny pup the day Velda and Damon brought Carly Mae home from the hospital. He looked like he'd been mauled by a bear, with gashes all over his body and one little ear torn off, but his eyes were bright and his energy high, so they let him in, tended to his wounds, and joked he was likely descended from the husky-sheltie pups that, according to local lore, had survived a drowning generations ago. He soon became the babe's constant companion and co-conspirator—a good thing since the twins were only mildly interested in their sister at the time. As the subject of her paintings, Buster was helping Carly Mae raise money for a new cause, the Touch of Kindness Rest Home, which was in danger of being shut down due to a leaky roof. She sold poses of her imperfect pooch on the sidewalk in front of the Kiminee Five 'N Dime for $1. There she caught the eye of Jasper Skrillpod, an art dealer passing through while on the hunt for antiques with his wife, Emily.

"Whoa! Look at that little girl painting right out there on the sidewalk." Jasper's unusually large brown eyes opened wide as he braked his Willy's wagon. "I've got to check her out. Look at her red-brown Heidi braids. And do you see that dog? What a Norman Rockwell scene."

Emily fanned herself with a flyer for a pancake breakfast she'd picked up in a nearby hamlet. "Do we have to stop? I don't feel well."

"You were fine just before we pulled into town. I wonder what happened." He brushed sandy blond bangs off his forehead.

Beads of sweat formed at Emily's temples and the nape of her neck, moistening her dark brown hair. "I don't know. I'm just overcome with nausea. It came on suddenly."

"I don't have to meet our little Picasso right now. We should go to the motel."

Knowing how much her husband loved introducing new talent to the art world, Emily decided to rally. "Maybe it'll pass if I just sit here while you go."

"Are you sure? I don't want this to bring on bad dreams tonight."

"You worry too much. I haven't had a nightmare in ages. Go on, go."

"Thanks, love." He leaned over and kissed her cheek. "I owe you one. I'll only be a minute." He exited the vehicle and strutted to Carly Mae. Five minutes later, he returned with a 7-Up. "Didn't see any Vernor's or Canada Dry inside, but this should help." He handed her the drink through the passenger window. "It looks like your color's coming back a bit."

"Thanks." Emily took a sip and closed her eyes. "I think my stomach has settled down some, and this is bound to help." She took a sip. "So what did you find out?"

"That sweet little girl, Carly Mae's her name, she'd love to see if I can sell her paintings, but I need to get parental permission. The mom's helping with inventory at the store, and Dusty, the young man working the cash register, said he'd fetch her."

Behind him, Velda stepped out of the Five 'N Dime. She straightened her pedal pushers, tucked in her sleeveless blouse, then patted down her disheveled brunette waves and stomped over to Carly Mae. "What's going on? You need my permission for some crazy thing?" she said to her daughter.

Carly Mae looked up from the canvas and frowned at the only mother in town who was always difficult to track down. "Where were you this time?" She dabbed a bit of white on Buster's ear.

"Now listen here, Carly Mae, you may be smart as a whip, but you have no call to question my whereabouts."

"I think the mother just arrived." Emily pointed toward Velda. "She's the spittin' image of Natalie Wood—well, a disheveled Natalie Wood."

Jasper turned his head and said, "Right you are. ... Bear with me, can you? I'll be quick as a wink."

"I'll do my best." Emily closed her eyes again and sipped more soda, relieved it was going down.

Twenty minutes later, Jasper returned and loaded five canvasses of Buster into the back of the wagon. "Sorry it took so long. That woman sure took some convincing. It was one question after another."

Emily wiped her palm across her moist forehead. "I've been okay so far, but I really need to get out of here and lie down."

Jasper slid into the driver's seat and started the engine. "We could cut the whole trip short and head back home."

"You wouldn't mind?"

"Of course not. You'll be home in case this turns out to be the flu coming on, and I'll get back to the gallery with these paintings. I don't know why, but I think they'll be a big hit."

They hurried home to Chicago, and within one week, Jasper sold all five paintings at his gallery for $25 apiece, keeping 70 percent of the proceeds for himself. Carly Mae's art soon became so popular, he sold her paintings at $75 a pop as fast as she could create them. He raised Carly Mae's cut to 50 percent when Damon complained. Carly Mae earned more than enough for the rest home's roof, so she funded new bay windows in the rec room, as well.

Several months into her art career, however, Carly Mae discarded painting in favor of playing a violin she found in her grandmother Missy's attic. Family lore goes that her great, great grandfather had marched it to and from the battlefront during the Civil War. He even hid it high in a hickory at Gettysburg, and retrieved it when the three-day bloodbath ended.

"Why are you throwing away your art for a squeaky violin?" her dad, Damon, asked. "You've never been particularly interested in music."

"I don't want to be some famous painter, Daddy. I only want to be me," she said.

Jasper, who envisioned championing Carly Mae all the way to international acclaim, pleaded with Damon to convince Carly Mae she simply had to keep painting. "People who have gifts most of us can only dream of have a responsibility to use them," he urged.

Damon backed up his daughter. "She's seven years old, a child. I'm not asking her to do anything except live by the Golden Rule. And who knows? She might be a gifted musician, too."

Velda sided with Jasper, but Carly Mae locked herself in her room and practiced the fiddle when her mom scolded her about the newfangled acrylic paints going to waste in the hall closet. Ever patient with his unpredictable wife, Damon got her to stretch out on the couch, massaged her perfect size six feet and asked her to try to remember what it was like to be a little girl. Ray and Blanche, precocious in their own right, took time out from preparing for a chess tournament to take their sister's side. They believed she should be able to do what she liked without everybody making a big fuss about it. Nevertheless, a fuss was made. Throughout town, from every curve and swimming hole along the Bendy River, each cornfield and every meadow, each business and every home, people had passionate discussions about Carly Mae, for she was the butter that anointed their morning toast, and while they knew she was Velda and Damon's daughter, they felt she was their very own.

Keep in Touch

I hope you enjoyed this excerpt from *The Kiminee Dream*. I expect to publish the book in 2020.

The best way to find out when it will be released is to join my readers group at https://lauramchaleholland.com.

If that's not your cup of tea, you can also join me on Facebook at https://www.facebook.com/Laura-McHale-Holland-Author, follow me on Twitter @lauramchh, and connect with me on Instagram @laura-mchh. I will welcome email from you, too, at laura@WORDforest.com.

www.ingramcontent.com/pod-product-compliance
Lightning Source LLC
Chambersburg PA
CBHW050157110726
47898CB00008B/2836